SPICY HOT COLORS
Colores Picantes

by Sherry Shahan
Illustrated by Paula Barragán

Red as chili sauce
Drip-drop
Spicy hot
Red as firecrackers
Snap! Bang!
Bebop Pop!
RED   ROJA

Colors explode off the page as Sherry Shahan's energetic, jazzy poetry introduces young readers to colors in English and Spanish. In a style brimming with rhythm and syncopation, Shahan introduces nine colors by interweaving images and dance steps. Ecuadoran artist Paula Barragán's computer-enhanced cut-paper illustrations capture the rhythm and vivacity of the text.

AUGUST HOUSE
Little Folk

August House Publishers, Inc.
ATLANTA
www.augusthouse.com

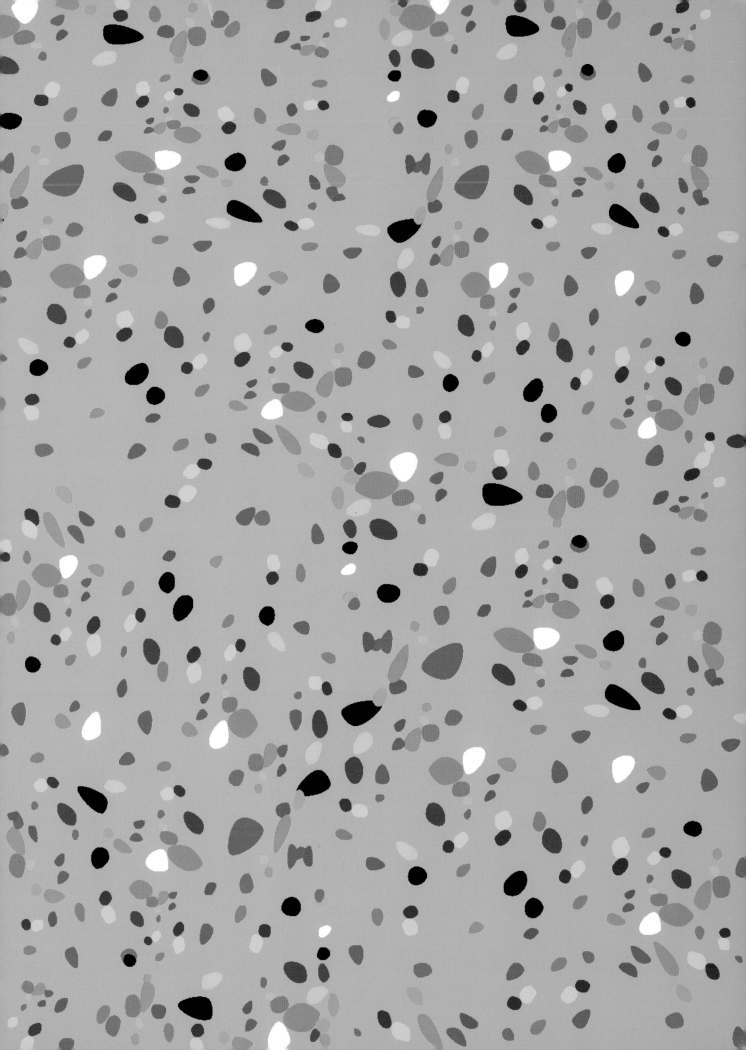

SHERRY SHAHAN
Illustrated by PAULA BARRAGÁN

AUGUST HOUSE
LittleFolk

Published 2004 by August House LittleFolk.

Atlanta. Georgia

www.augusthouse.com

Book design by Mina Greenstein

Manufactured in Korea

10   9   8   7   6   5   PB

LIBRARY OF CONGRESS CATALOGING-IN-PUBLICATION DATA

Shahan, Sherry.

Spicy hot colors: colores picantes / Sherry Shahan ; illustrated by Paula Berragán.

p. cm.

English and Spanish.

ISBN 978-0-87483-815-2 PB

ISBN 978-0-87483-741-4 HB

1. Colors. 2. Colors - Psychological aspects. I. Barragán. Paula. 1963- II. Title.

QC495.8.S53 2004

535.6 - dc22   2004040990

First Hardcover Edition. 2004

First Paperback Edition. 2007

The paper used in this publication meets the minimum requirements of the

American National Standards for Information Sciences

Permanence of Paper for Printed Library Materials. ANSI.48

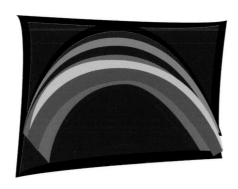

For my mother, Sylvia, and
two daughters,
Kristina Michelle and Kyle Shannon.
con amor
—SS

For Pablo—XO
—PB

Red as chili sauce
Drip-drop
Spicy hot

Red as firecrackers
Snap! Bang!
Bebop Pop!

RED   ROJO

Orange as sarapes
Sizzling lap wraps

Orange as roosters
Flitter-flutter
Flap!

ORANGE ANARANJADO

Yellow as gourds
 spitter-sputter seeds
Yellow as cobs of corn
 hip-hoppin' treat
YELLOW AMARILLO

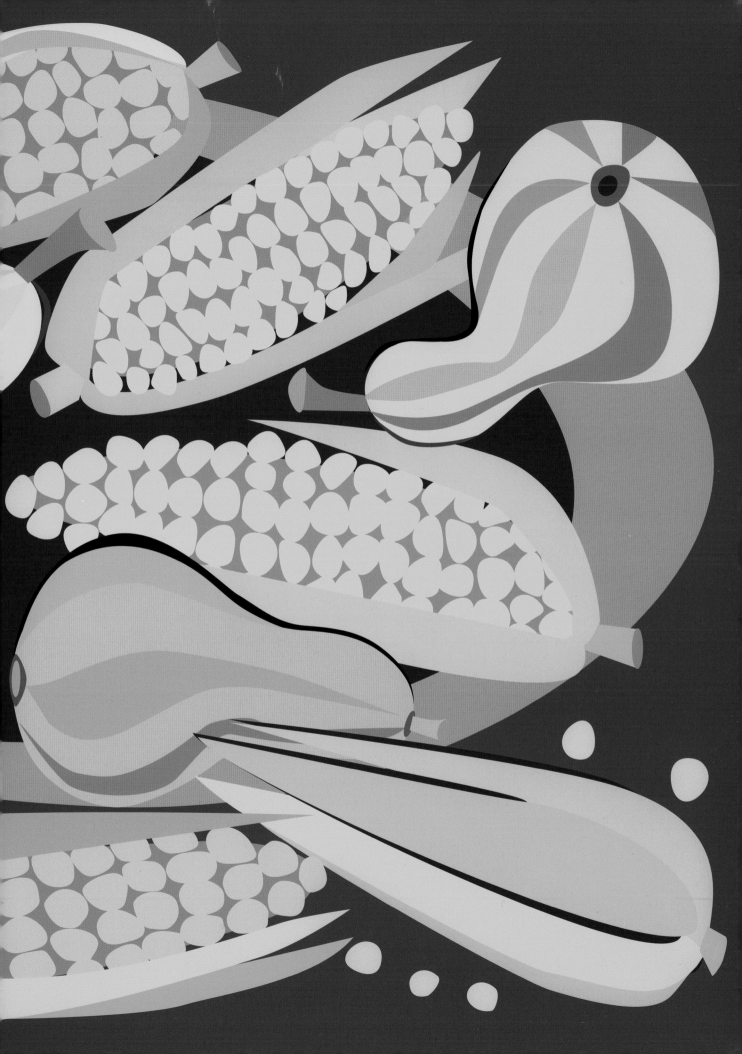

Green as Mexican iguanas
Slither
Slide
Samba!

Green as cilantro and cactus
Wiggle
Waggle
Rumba!

GREEN   VERDE

Purple as piñatas
Smack! Whack!
Spin on the ground

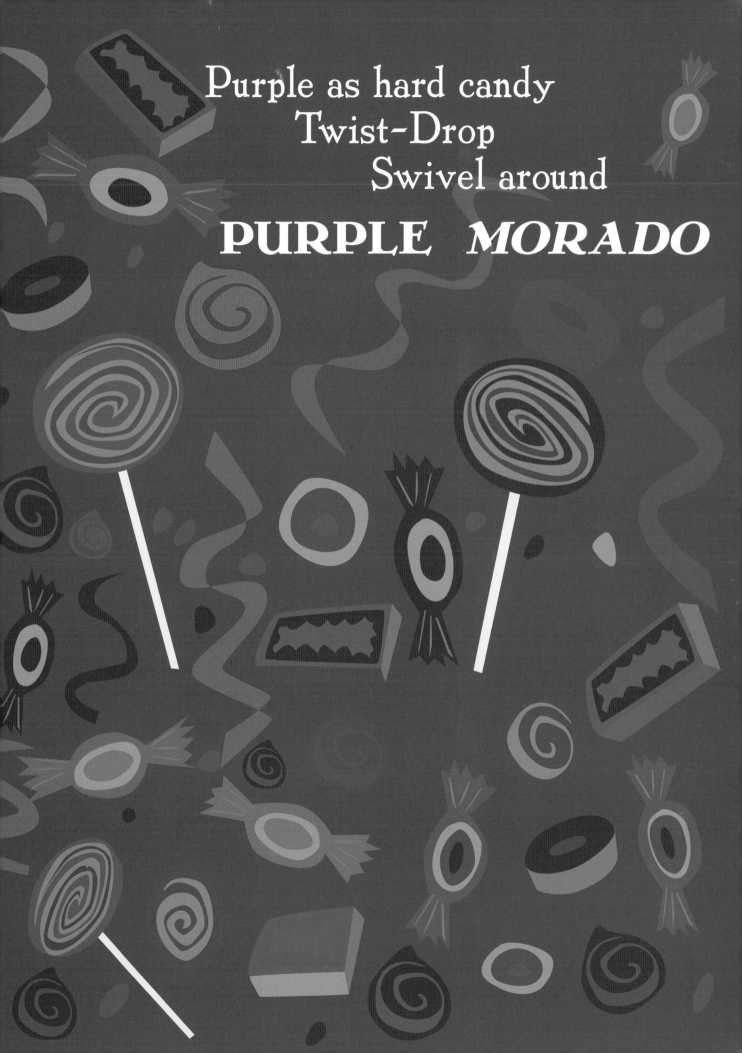

Purple as hard candy
Twist-Drop
Swivel around

PURPLE *MORADO*

Blue as tin angels
zinging on a string

Blue as paper dragons
Boogie-woogie
Swing!

BLUE *AZUL*

Brown as buñuelos
a crisp crunchy sound

Black as castanets
clickety-clickety
clack-clack

Black as boot heels
rat-a-tat
Flick-flack
BLACK   NEGRO

White as sombreros
heel-toe hat dances

White as toy skeletons
rattle-rap
Razzmatazz!

WHITE

BLANCO

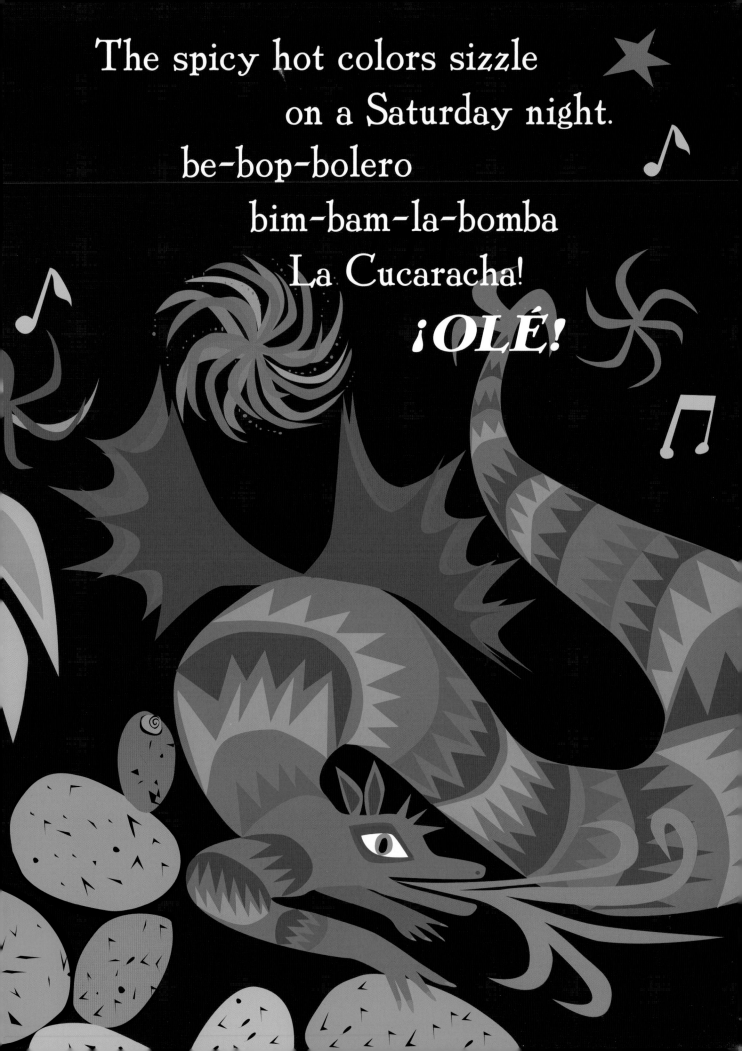

The spicy hot colors sizzle
on a Saturday night.
be-bop-bolero
bim-bam-la-bomba
La Cucaracha!
¡OLÉ!

VOCABULARY

Buñuelos Puffs of fried dough sprinkled with sugar and cinnamon.

Cactus A spiny plant that grows in hot, dry regions.

Castanets A pair of small shell-shaped instruments held in the hand. One shell is clicked against the other.

Cilantro The lacy leaves of this herb are used to flavor spicy dishes.

La Cucaracha A world-famous Mexican song about a cockroach.

Mexican hat dance A traditional heel-and-toe dance stepped around a *sombrero*.

Mexican iguana A large green lizard.

Paper dragons and tin angels
Playful decorations used in festivals.

Piñata A brightly colored papier-mâché container filled with candy, fruit, and toys. Children are blindfolded and given a stick to break the piñata, which is hung above their heads.

Sarape A colorful shawl or blanket.

Skeletons Used in a festival called Day of the Dead. Despite its name, it isn't a spooky time, like Halloween. Participants celebrate loved ones who are no longer living.

Sombrero A broad-brimmed hat worn in the southwestern United States, Mexico, and Spain.

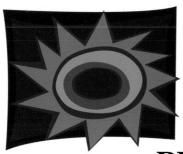

PRONUNCIATION

Amarillo (ah-mah-REEL-yoh)
Anaranjado (ah-nah-rahn-HA-do)
Azul (ah-SOOL)
Blanco (BLAHN-koh)
Buñuelos (Boo-NYWAH-los)
La Cucaracha (la koo-ka-RA-cha)
Morado (mor-RAH-do)
Negro (NEH-groh)
Olé (o-LEH)
Pardo (PAHR-doh)
Piñata (pee-NYA-ta)
Rojo (ROH-hoh)
Sarape (ser-RAH-pay)
Sombreros (sohm-BREH-ros)
Verde (VEHR-deh)

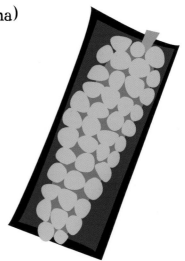

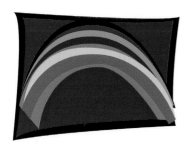

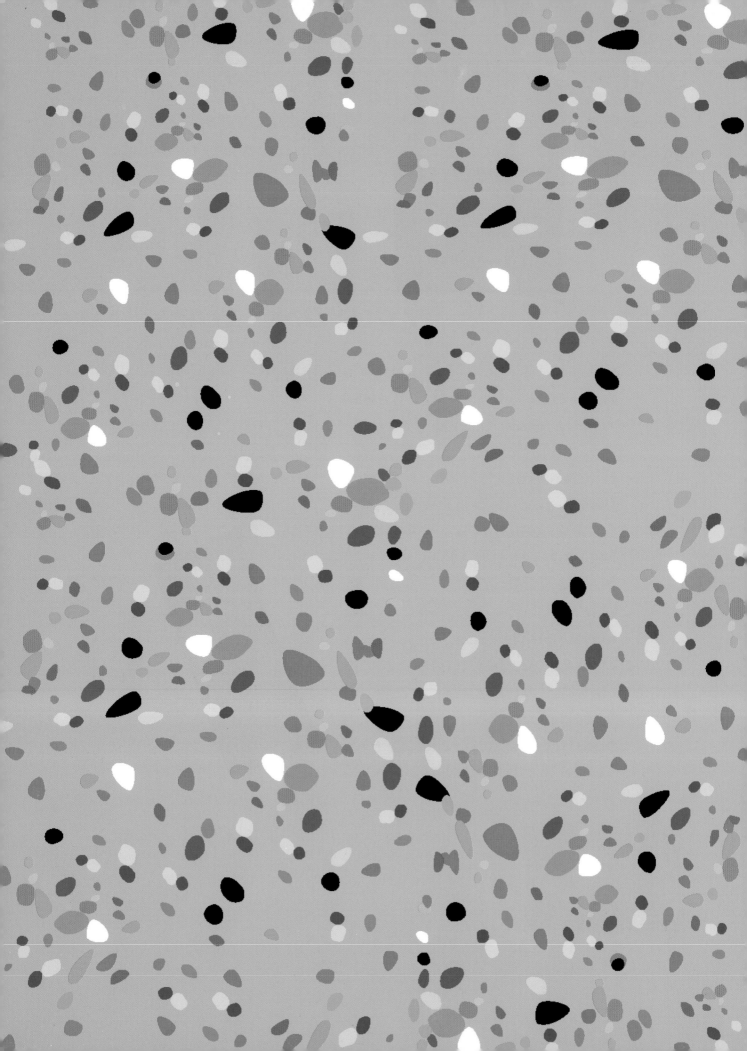

Writer and photo-illustrator **SHERRY SHAHAN** has published more than twenty children's fiction and nonfiction books. Her previous picture books include *Jazzy Alphabet* and *Feeding Time at the Zoo*, and she is currently reteaming with Paula Barragán on the forthcoming *Cool Cats Counting*. She lives in Cayucos, California.

PAULA BARRAGÁN is a native of Quito, Ecuador. Her first picture book, *Love to Mamá*, received starred reviews in *Kirkus* and *School Library Journal* and was included in Chicago Public Library's Best of the Best List, Bank Street College of Education's Best Children's Books of the Year, and Notable Social Studies Trade Books for Young People.

Jacket illustration©2004 by Paula Barragan

Manufactured in Korea